The Dame
Is Bored

©Published 2022.
BookLife Publishing Ltd.
King's Lynn, Norfolk PE30 4LS

ISBN 978-1-80155-150-2

The Dame is Bored
Written by John Wood, Adapted by William Anthony
Illustrated by Simona Hodonova

An Introduction to Accessible Readers...

Our 'really readable' Accessible Readers have been specifically created to support the reading development of young readers with learning differences, such as dyslexia.

Our aim is to share our love of books with children, providing the same learning and developmental opportunities to every child.

INCREASED FONT SIZE AND SPACING improves readability and ensures text feels much less crowded.

OFF-WHITE BACKGROUNDS ON MATTE PAPER improves text contrast and avoids dazzling readers.

SIMPLIFIED PAGE LAYOUT reduces distractions and aids concentration.

CAREFULLY CRAFTED along guidelines set out in the British Dyslexia Association's Dyslexia-Friendly Style Guide.

The Dame
Is Bored

Written by John Wood
Illustrated by Simona Hodonova

The Dame of Faketown was fed up. She was stuck inside on another boring day. Other people were walking outside. They were joyful.

"What's wrong, Dame?" asked the cleaner.

The Dame had an idea. She felt strange. Then she felt excited. She grinned and jumped up from her chair.

"No one is allowed to walk on the ground!" she said.

The Dame ran out of the room, shouting all the way. This was a great idea. It was even better than the Big Homework Fire (and that was a brilliant idea)!

The Dame of Faketown ran to the roof. All the people below looked up at her.

"From now on, no one is allowed to walk on the ground!" she yelled.

The townspeople were scared. Their eyes were wide. They had no idea what to do.

"No way!" said one person.

"Is that safe?" asked another.

"This is not good at all!" screamed one man.

"You can't do that!" yelled the man's mother.

"Where did you learn to be a dame?" shouted the man's mother's brother.

But the Dame of Faketown didn't listen. She jumped into her plane and flew into the air.

"And if you do go on the ground, I will send you to prison forever!"

The townspeople all looked for a place to go. The baker climbed a tree. The postwoman sat on her van. The teacher didn't know where to go, so she sat on the fence.

"Quick! To the playground!" said the children. "We will be safe there!"

They perched on the swings and they climbed on the monkey bars.

They balanced on the seesaw and they held onto the roundabout. There was no time to waste. They sat on the slide, but that was not a good idea!

"This is silly!" said the headteacher, swinging from a rope.

"Very silly," said the zookeeper, hanging on to a bird. "Someone needs to say something to the Dame and put a stop to this."

"My cakes are burning. I blame the Dame!" said the cakemaker.

"That shop is burning. I blame the Dame!" said the firefighter.

A big hot air balloon rose into the air. The school teacher was inside. She was going to get the Dame to sort all this mess out.

"I'm coming too," shouted the headteacher.

The headteacher did a big swing on the rope. He flew high in the air and reached out for the hot air balloon.

The headteacher missed the hot air balloon. In fact, he didn't even get close. It was a good try, though. He fell a long, long way down.

"It's all right," yelled the headteacher. "I've landed in a tree. I didn't go on the ground!"

The wind whisked the teacher's balloon off into the sunset.

The balloon chased the Dame's plane beyond the clouds in the sky.

"Please, stop all of this," said the teacher. "This really is no way for a dame to behave."

"Never! I'm having way too much fun!" yelled the Dame.

But then there was a big scream from below. They both looked down.

It was Baz the baker. He was at the top of a tall tree and it was swaying in the strong wind. It was going to snap any second.

"Don't worry, I will save you!"
shouted the Dame of Faketown.

The plane dived out of the sky.
It chugged and chattered as it flew
towards the ground.

The tree was swaying even more. The baker screamed. The teacher did not know how to make a hot air balloon go downwards. Everyone gasped. Was the Dame too late?

The plane swooped down, and the Dame caught the baker as he fell out of the swaying tree. She had made it just in time!

They landed, safe on the ground. Everyone cheered. The baker and Dame were rather dazed.

"What a day," said the postwoman. "But can we please go back on the ground now?"

The Dame nodded.

"Yes, I think that sounds perfect," she said with a smile and a nod.

The next day, people's feet were planted firmly to the ground. They were all joyful. It was all back to the way it was.

But the Dame was fed up again.
She tapped her fingers and feet.
Then, she smiled. She was thinking
of a new idea.

The cleaner shook his head.

"I'm moving to another town,"
he said.

The Dame Is Bored: Quiz

1. What is the Dame's best idea ever?

2. Where did the children go?

    (a) The playground
    (b) Home
    (c) The shops

3. Who did the Dame save from the top of a tall tree?

4. How do the people of Faketown feel about the Dame?

5. How would you have avoided touching the ground if you lived in Faketown?

Helpful Hints for Reading at Home

This 'really readable' Accessible Reader has been carefully written and designed to help children with learning differences whether they are reading in the classroom or at home. However, there are some extra ways in which you can help your child at home.

- Try to provide a quiet space for your child to read, with as few distractions as possible.

- Try to allow your child as much time as they need to decode the letters and words on the page.

- Reading with a learning difference can be frustrating and difficult. Try to let your child take short, managed breaks between reading sessions if they begin to feel frustrated.

- Build your child's confidence with positive praise and encouragement throughout.

- Your child's teacher, as well as many charities, can provide you with lots of tips and techniques to help your child read at home.